The
BROKEN
DRAGON

KAREN McCOMBIE

Illustrated by
Anneli Bray

Barrington Stoke

For Aidan and his groovy granny Wendy!

First published in 2023 in Great Britain by
Barrington Stoke Ltd
18 Walker Street, Edinburgh, EH3 7LP

www.barringtonstoke.co.uk

Text © 2023 Karen McCombie
Illustrations © 2023 Anneli Bray

The moral right of Karen McCombie and Anneli Bray to be identified as the author and illustrator of this work has been asserted in accordance with the Copyright, Designs and Patents Act, 1988

A CIP catalogue record for this book is available from the British Library upon request

ISBN: 978-1-80090-186-5

Printed by Hussar Books, Poland

The
BROKEN
DRAGON

CONTENTS

CHAPTER 1

Hunting for dragons with Nan!

Tyra and her nan are in their favourite place – the Second Chance charity shop.

"Nan! Look at this, Nan!" Tyra calls out. Tyra is small for her age (nearly 10) but makes up for it with a very loud voice and very interesting clothes.

"What have you found?" asks Nan. Then she smiles when she sees the white egg cup that Tyra is holding up. It has two little feet in a pair of red boots.

"Ooh, that's cute!" says Nan.

Both of them know they won't be buying it. Back at Nan's, Tyra already has a great egg cup that looks like a hippo. But it's always fun to see what they can find in charity shops. *They're more like treasure shops*, Tyra thinks.

Tyra moved in with her nan at the start of summer, and sometimes Nan doesn't have much money. So they buy things when Nan can afford it and enjoy looking at stuff the rest of the time.

But there's one type of treasure that Tyra is always on the hunt for – dragons!

Tyra is mad about dragons. And since she moved in with Nan, thanks to all their charity-shop hunting, she has more and more dragon treasure.

So far Tyra has found ...

- five books with dragons on the cover

- a 1,000-piece dragon puzzle (that's kind of hard)

- dragon Top Trump cards

- a silver dragon necklace

- a dragon egg (sort of rubbery and see-through with a baby dragon asleep inside)

- a Lego dragon (with a few bits missing but that's OK)

- two T-shirts with dragons on the front.

There are no dragons in the Second Chance shop today, but Nan spots something else.

"Hey, this would suit you!" says Nan, pointing to a beanie hat with rainbow stripes. "It has a hole in it, but I could fix that. And look at these trainers – they're a size too big, but you could wear them with thick socks till they fit you."

"I love them!" says Tyra. The beanie hat looks so cute. And the trainers are a really nice bright green. They'd look great with the red laces from her old trainers.

"Let's get them both!" says Nan. "You can wear them to school on Monday!"

Suddenly, Tyra stops feeling happy.

It has been so fun starting a new life with Nan. But starting at a brand-new school is kind of scary.

Tyra knows that she's a loud and bouncy person, and sometimes people think she's **too much**. And sometimes people think her dragon treasures are **too weird**.

What will it be like at the new school? Will everyone think she's **too much** and **too weird**, like they did at her last school ...?

CHAPTER 2

Trying to be brave

Tyra and Nan wait outside the playground. There is a lot of noise from all the children and their grown-ups.

At least no one wears school uniform here, thinks Tyra. At her old school she had to wear a white shirt and grey trousers, and there were always grubby marks on them.

But today she's wearing her favourite T-shirt. It has a baby dragon on it, flying through pink clouds. The top goes great with her baggy tie-dye shorts, green trainers and new rainbow beanie.

"Are you excited?" asks Nan, giving Tyra's hand a squeeze.

"Yes!" says Tyra.

Holding Nan's hand makes Tyra feel safe and strong.

And squeezed tight in the palm of Tyra's *other* hand is a tiny plastic dragon called Flame. Tyra found Flame in the street one day and didn't want to leave him lost and lonely there on the pavement, like litter. Nan washed Flame clean in the sink back at home till he looked good as new.

Tyra hopes her new teacher will let Flame sit on her table. Tyra also hopes her new school friends will like her outfit and that they will want to play with her dragon Top Trump cards at break-time.

Most of all, Tyra hopes Flame will help her be brave all day, when she doesn't have Nan's hand to hold.

As Tyra and Nan walk into the playground, Nan bends down and whispers something in Tyra's ear.

"What do we do when we feel nervous?" she asks.

Tyra knows exactly what Nan means. They look at each other with big grins. They take deep breaths at the same time and let out a great big dragon ...

"ROAAAARRRRR!!!"

And everyone in the playground turns round.

CHAPTER 3

Being the new kid is hard

Tyra's first day at school is a big muddle of different things. It's exciting but tiring. It's good but hard.

There are so many new people to get to know and so many new names to learn. Even the teacher's name is tricky – Mrs Suzuki.

Mrs Suzuki writes it on the white board, and Tyra reads it lots of times and whispers it over and over to herself.

And then, "**Mrs SUZUKI!**" Tyra bursts out. She didn't mean the shout to happen, or for her voice to be so loud. But the teacher just smiles and nods at her. All her classmates grin and look at each other.

Then there are all the questions.

"Why have you come to this school?" one girl asks at break-time. Everyone is standing round Tyra, waiting for her to answer.

"**Because I moved here to live with my nan,**" says Tyra.

"Why do you live with your nan?" someone asks.

"**Just because I do!**" says Tyra.

"Why do you wear such funny clothes?" asks a boy.

"**Because they're more interesting!**" says Tyra. She does a dance that makes her baggy tie-dye shorts flap-flap.

"How come you have so much dragon stuff?" asks a girl.

"Dragons are just really cool!" says Tyra, holding up her Top Trump cards so everyone can see the pictures on them.

Another boy asks a question.

"Why did you and your nan make that roaring noise this morning?"

"Cos it's fun – try it!" Tyra takes a breath and is about to roar again. But then she sees that even more children have come to look, and they are in a big circle all around her. Maybe her roar is scary? Tyra lets the roar slip away.

Then she spots that one girl from her class is wearing a big badge with "10" on it.

"Hey, it's your birthday!" Tyra bursts out.

Tyra holds up Flame and sings the "Happy Birthday" song in a baby dragon voice. She stops at the bit where you say the person's name, because she can't remember what the girl is called.

She hears some giggling and then a grown-up voice.

"Everyone ready to get back to class?" asks Mrs Suzuki. The bell has rung. Tyra is glad to go inside, where everyone has to stare at the teacher and not at her.

At lunch-time, Tyra follows the other children to the dinner hall but doesn't know where to sit. So Tyra asks a nice lady where the girls' toilets are. She doesn't really need to go, but she finds a bench where no one can see her, and she plonks herself down and opens her plastic lunchbox.

The weird thing is, her tummy has shrunk. All she can eat is one bite of her sandwich and three cheese-and-onion crisps.

She looks at Flame, who is sitting on her banana.

"Being new is tricky," she whispers to him.

CHAPTER 4

Home time – or is it?

When the bell for the end of school rings, Tyra is very happy to see Nan in the playground with all the other grown-ups.

"**Nan!**" she shouts out as she runs.

Nan waves, but she is busy talking to a smiley woman wearing a long straight dress, silky trousers and a hijab as blue as the sky.

Tyra runs over and wraps her arms around Nan. Nan's bobbly big cardi tickles Tyra's nose and makes her smile.

"Hello, my darling!" says Nan. "Have you had a good day?"

"Mmm," mumbles Tyra. All she wants to do is go home to the flat. She wants to flop on the sofa, eat some toast and watch her favourite anime show – *Drago-Bot*! It stars a creature that is part dragon, part robot, who flies a spaceship around different galaxies and has excellent adventures.

"Can we go now, Nan?" Tyra asks loudly, yawning at the same time.

Nan doesn't seem to hear.

"Tyra, this is Yasmeen's mum," says Nan, and she nods at the lady next to her.

"Hello, I'm Tyra!" says Tyra, in her best, loudest, most friendly voice.

"Hi, Tyra!" smiles the lady with the sky-blue hijab. "It's my daughter Yasmeen's birthday today and we're having a picnic in the park. The whole class will be there. Do you want to come?"

Tyra looks over at the girl with the number 10 badge. She's in the middle of a group of boys and girls, all chattering and laughing.

"Isn't that kind? Won't that be fun?" says Nan, then she gives Tyra a soft prod with her elbow.

The prod means Tyra should say something. Tyra was thinking about the birthday picnic, and she forgot her manners.

"Thank you!" Tyra says at last. She gives Yasmeen's mum a big smile. Nan always says that Tyra's smiles are pure gold.

And Tyra is suddenly feeling bright and shiny inside and not even a tiny bit tired any more!

CHAPTER 5

The picnic and the present

Tyra and Nan are late getting to the picnic. They stopped at the shops to get Yasmeen a present.

Tyra doesn't really know Yasmeen yet, so she asked Nan to buy something everyone likes – an extra-big bar of chocolate.

"Excited?" Nan asks Tyra as they walk into the sunshiney park.

"Yes!" says Tyra.

They both see the big circle of adults and children sitting on colourful picnic blankets.

And then Tyra spots Yasmeen.

"Nan – Yasmeen is opening her presents already!" Tyra says.

"Well, let's get over there!" says Nan, and together they hurry across the grass.

Yasmeen's mum smiles and waves, but everyone else is busy watching Yasmeen rip open all her presents.

Tyra and Nan sit down on the edge of a blanket, ready to join in with all the oohs and ahhs.

Yasmeen is holding up a huge book about the Egyptians with an amazing gold cover. Next she gets a big letter Y made of lightbulbs that she can put on her bedroom wall. She unwraps paint sets and craft kits and lots of vouchers for cool shops. She gets a mobile phone from her mum, and everyone makes jealous noises. Then a lady passes Yasmeen a big box wrapped in shiny paper.

"Thank you, Auntie Zainab!" says Yasmeen.

Tyra jumps to her feet when she sees what the present is.

"Drago-Bot!" Tyra shouts out. **"Hey, it's Drago-Bot!!"**

It's the most amazing toy from the TV show. Tyra's seen ads for it.

It's not a toy for little kids – it's called an "animatronic", and it's the sort of thing grown-up fans of *Drago-Bot* love too. It lifts its wings, roars and has flashing red eyes. It even says lines from the show when you talk to it. Another thing Tyra knows about this toy is that it's very, very expensive.

Everyone is crowding around Yasmeen and her Drago-Bot, and Tyra can't see either of them any more.

And suddenly things don't feel right.

It's hot today, and Tyra has been holding the giant chocolate bar in her hand all this time. It's started to go all squishy and oozy. Yasmeen has had some great presents, and Tyra can't exactly go over and give her a melty rectangle of gloop.

Tyra goes hot and cold. Her tummy feels too tight and too loose at the same time, like there's a knot inside her.

"Are you OK, Tyra?" she hears Nan ask.

"I feel a bit sick," says Tyra in a very small voice. "I think I'd like to go home."

Nan puts her hand on Tyra's forehead. Then she notices the bendy chocolate bar and gently takes it from Tyra and puts it in her bag.

"Are you sure you wouldn't like to stay a bit longer?" says Nan.

"No thank you," Tyra says nicely, and slips her hand into Nan's.

Even though the sun is still shining, even though nothing is wrong, Tyra has stopped feeling bright and shiny inside.

CHAPTER 6

Nan's surprise

Tyra and Nan are nearly back at the flat.

"You haven't said much, Tyra," says Nan as she gets her keys out of her bag. "Still feeling sick?"

"No," says Tyra, holding Flame in her fist. The tips of his hard wings are digging into her hand.

Tyra doesn't feel sick any more. But she does feel odd.

All the way home from the park she's been thinking about stuff. Tricky stuff.

Stuff like ...

- Yasmeen's mum had invited Tyra to the birthday picnic. Did Yasmeen even want her there?

- All the grown-ups at the picnic were much younger than Nan.

- All the grown-ups were dressed smarter and neater than Nan.

- All the boys and girls were dressed smarter and neater than Tyra.

- When Tyra's new classmates giggled at her in school today, was it because they thought she was funny or silly? Funny and silly are very different things.

- Did all the girls and boys think Tyra was **too much** and **too weird**?

Tyra takes off her new rainbow beanie so she can think better and follows Nan into the flat.

"Stop there, Tyra!" Nan says just before they get to the living room. "Close your eyes and take two steps forward ... I have a surprise for you!"

The tricky stuff vanishes as Tyra gets excited. What does Nan mean?

Tyra does as she's told and closes her eyes.

She moves forward, with Nan helping her.

"OK, you can look now!"

Tyra opens her eyes. Nan has taken her over to the table in the corner of the living room. On the table there are three things – a pile of ironing to put away, a bottle of ketchup and something completely amazing!

"**Wow!**" is the only word Tyra can manage.

On the table is the most perfect dragon.

It's white as snow, with wings held out wide. It has a long lizard tail and big claws that rest on a piece of grey rock. Every single bit of this dragon is wonderful. You can see each tiny scale, each ripple on the wings.

The dragon has nostrils that you can picture smoke puffing out of. It has orange eyes that look like glimmers of fire.

"**Wow!**" Tyra says again, running her fingers along the open wings.

"I spotted it in the Second Chance shop window today," says Nan. "I knew I had to get it for you! It's a present to celebrate your first day at your new school. Do you like it?"

"Thank you so much, Nan! I love it!" Tyra yelps, finding her voice and her words again. "I need to think of a really good name for it ..."

"And we'll have to think of where to put it," says Nan. "We could make space for it in here, or put it on the shelf in your bedroom."

Tyra stops listening to what Nan's saying. She's even forgotten about finding a name for her new dragon. That's because she's just had the best idea ever!

CHAPTER 7

The terrible trip

The next morning on the way to school, Tyra is so excited. Her chest feels packed full of balloons that could pop at any moment.

She's wearing her favourite outfit – a black T-shirt with the best-ever dragon on it. It's really fierce looking and flapping its huge wings. It's really an adult's top, so for Tyra it's like a baggy dress, and she has some great red leggings on too, which match the dragon's breath of fire.

Yesterday, Tyra wasn't sure that she fitted in at her new school, but today is going to be different, and it's all thanks to Snowy the Snow Dragon!

"Do you want me to take a turn?" asks Nan, holding out her arms as they walk.

But Tyra holds on tight to her snow-white dragon.

"No, I'm fine! Snowy isn't heavy at all!" says Tyra, even though her arms are getting tired.

She can't wait for everyone to see Snowy. She can't wait till everyone is crowding around her, wow-ing about how wonderful her dragon is. She's even made up a story about Snowy and an adventure he's been on. Tyra will tell it to her classmates, and they'll all want to be friends with her!

"Look, I'm still not sure this is a good idea, Tyra," says Nan as they go into the playground. "Snowy might break ..."

"But I'll take good care of him, Nan! I promise!" says Tyra. She holds on to her dragon even tighter. Her fingers are starting to go numb. **"Oh, look – there's Mrs Suzuki!"**

Tyra speeds up when she spots her teacher. Mrs Suzuki is standing near the main door chatting to a few of the boys and girls in Tyra's class. Wait till they see what Tyra has to show them! Yasmeen's Drago-Bot is great and can do clever electronic tricks, but it isn't as stunning and special as Snowy the Snow Dragon.

"Tyra – slow down!" Nan calls out, but Tyra is already running over to Mrs Suzuki and the others and doesn't listen.

"What have you got there, Tyra?" asks Mrs Suzuki.

"Wow!" say all the children around her. Some of them are already reaching out to touch and stroke the dragon figure.

"This is Snowy the Snow Dragon!" Tyra says proudly.

"Snowy?" says one of the boys. The way he says it shows that he doesn't think much of the name.

Tyra stops feeling so excited. The truth is she's not sure about the name either. She's spent hours trying to find the perfect name for her splendid white dragon, but nothing sounded right.

At bedtime she'd looked at Flame in case
he'd help her think up an awesome name, but
it was no good. Maybe he was grumpy cos
Tyra liked the new dragon more.

Then she hears her teacher say something.

"Did you know that in Japan there are
lots of stories about snow dragons?" says Mrs
Suzuki.

"Are there?" says Tyra.

"Yes! And one famous snow dragon is
called 'Okami'," Mrs Suzuki explains.

Tyra looks at the dragon in her arms. She
looks into his sparkling orange eyes and says,
"Okami".

Tyra is almost sure the dragon blinks.

"That's it! Okami is his name!" says Tyra.

She suddenly spots Yasmeen out of the corner of her eye and turns to show her Okami.

"Yasmeen!" Tyra calls out. "I have a dragon too! His name is—"

The only pair of clean socks Tyra could find this morning were thin ones with ladybirds on them. They're slippy inside her too-big green trainers. And Tyra was so keen to get to school that she didn't tie her red laces very well. So when Tyra turns round, her feet tip and twist and she trips.

And as she tips and twists and trips, Tyra sees and hears things happen. But they're happening in slow motion.

Voices are shouting, "NO!"

Arms are coming out to stop Tyra falling.

Yasmeen runs forward to catch Okami the dragon as he sails through the air, his wings spread out.

She's too late. Tyra's knees and elbows crunch onto the hard tarmac. And *CRACK!!*

Tyra's dragon hits the ground. The terrible sound makes Tyra's heart miss a beat.

CHAPTER 8

Sore and sad

Pain stings everywhere, but Tyra doesn't even notice.

She's too busy picking up the pieces of her broken dragon.

"I'm sorry, Nan!" Tyra sobs. **"I did try to be careful!"**

"Shh, it doesn't matter," says Nan, dabbing at Tyra's bleeding knee with a tissue.

Everyone crowds round them, looking sad and sorry for Tyra and her dragon.

"It was so cool!" she hears one of the boys say. He passes her a piece of claw that she missed.

The school bell is ringing. But Tyra is too upset to get up.

"Listen, Tyra," says Mrs Suzuki, who is kneeling down beside her. "I have an idea. I know how we can fix Okami."

Mrs Suzuki takes the broken pieces of the dragon out of Tyra's hands. Tyra counts nine different pieces, some big and some small.

"But **how** can you fix him?" Tyra sniffs as Nan helps her stand up. Nan ties the red laces of the trainers extra tight so there will be no more tips and twists and trips.

"Trust me ..." says Mrs Suzuki. She walks off, and Tyra and the rest of the class follow.

Yasmeen puts her arm around Tyra's waist and helps her limp into school.

Another girl has Tyra's backpack with her lunchbox inside.

A boy is saying something about getting the first-aid kit.

"It'll be all right!" Tyra can hear Nan calling out from behind her.

Tyra is sore and sad and can't see how it'll be all right.

But then again, everyone being so nice makes her feel a little bit better.

CHAPTER 9

How to fix a broken dragon

Tyra is sitting at her table with the bits of her broken dragon in front of her.

Someone has cleaned her bashed elbow and knees and put plasters on them. She's holding an icepack on the knee that hurts the most. The boys made her laugh by saying she'll have the coolest bruises ever!

And now everyone is listening to what Mrs Suzuki has planned for the broken dragon.

"Maybe she's a witch and can magic it back together!" whispers a girl called Scarlett.

"I wish she was a witch and *could* do that!" Tyra whispers back.

"I'm not a witch, Tyra, but I can do something magical!" says Mrs Suzuki.

Tyra blushes. She's a loud sort of person who needs to whisper more softly.

Mrs Suzuki is smiling, which makes Tyra feel better. And now she's pointing to a word that's popped up on the board.

The word is *KINTSUGI*.

Everyone in class says the word softly, all at different times. Tyra thinks it sounds a bit like rain pattering on a window.

"*Kintsugi* is the Japanese art of mending broken things," Mrs Suzuki explains. "But it's a very special sort of mending. It means the bits are glued together with gold!"

Mrs Suzuki shows them a picture of a grey bowl that is criss-crossed with golden lines.

"Japanese people believe that *kintsugi* makes an object more unique and more special than it was before."

Tyra isn't sure what unique means and is too shy to ask. She doesn't want to look silly in front of the class.

"Miss, what does unique mean?" asks a boy called Freddie.

"Good question!" says Mrs Suzuki. "It means there's nothing else like it. Think about how many plain grey bowls there are. But this bowl is so special, with its very own gold markings that follow the cracks!"

Tyra gasps. She suddenly understands what Mrs Suzuki is going to do.

"You're going to mend my dragon with gold?" she bursts out.

"Well, our school hasn't got any real gold," says Mrs Suzuki with a big smile. "But we can use glue and gold paint! We're going to get started and fix Okami."

Tyra hears her classmates hiss "Yessss!" and sees some of them punch the air. Yasmeen even starts a chant.

"Kintsugi! Kintsugi! Kintsugi!"

As Mrs Suzuki gets the glue and the gold paint and some very thin paintbrushes out, the chant gets louder and louder.

"KINTSUGI! KINTSUGI! KINTSUGI!" Tyra sing-songs along with her classmates.

As the fun new word bounces around the classroom, it feels like all the upset of the morning is being mended.

CHAPTER 10

A warm glow inside

When Nan comes to meet Tyra, everything is very different from the morning.

Tyra is smiling and chatting with her new friends in the playground. But she smiles even more when she sees Nan.

"Nan! Look, Nan! *Kintsugi* saved Okami!" Tyra calls out, and she holds up her dragon.

Nan looks puzzled. She's surprised to see the snow dragon in one piece.

And Tyra can tell Nan didn't understand what she just said.

"Have you been learning a new language at school today?" asks Nan, coming over to inspect the snow dragon.

"No!" laughs Tyra. **"Okami is the proper name of my dragon. And *kintsugi* is a Japanese word for when you mend things with gold."**

"It makes broken things more beautiful and special," Scarlett tells Nan.

"Unique," says Freddie, remembering the word he learned today.

"You are so lucky to have this, Tyra," says Yasmeen, gently touching Okami's gold-streaked wing. "I wish it was mine!"

"Oh my goodness, that dragon's lovely!" says Yasmeen's mum, who's just arrived along with lots of other grown-ups. "And you know what else is lovely? Your beanie hat, Tyra. Yasmeen wants me to knit one just like it for her!"

"I'm going to ask my granny to knit one for me too!" says Scarlett.

Tyra feels a warm glow inside. Maybe at this new school people don't think she's **too much** or **too weird**?

"There'll be rainbows bobbing around the playground in no time!" Nan jokes. "But it's been a long day. Shall we get you home, Tyra?"

Tyra nods, waves bye to her friends and walks towards the gates with Nan. Suddenly she feels shy. There's a question she needs to ask.

"Are you cross with me for breaking Okami?" asks Tyra in a small voice.

"Of course not! Accidents happen," Nan replies. "And like you say, your dragon is even more special now. You can treasure him just the way he is. Just like I treasure you!"

"But I'm not special or mended with gold!" Tyra laughs.

"Yes, but some things just shine from the inside. You can't always see the gold," says Nan, and she bends down to kiss the top of Tyra's head.

Tyra isn't sure what Nan means. But at that moment a loud noise makes her look back into the playground.

"ARRRGHH!"

The shouty "arrrghh" noise is coming from Freddie and some of the other boys.

"Oh! I think they're trying to roar like dragons!" Tyra says in surprise.

"Well, they're not doing it right, are they?" says Nan. "How about we show them how it's done?"

Nan smiles at Tyra. Tyra grins at Nan.

And together they do a great big dragon ...

"ROAAAARRRRR!!!"

Our books are tested
for children and young people by
children and young people.

Thanks to everyone who consulted on
a manuscript for their time and effort in
helping us to make our books better
for our readers.